Richmond upon Thames Libraries

Renew online at www.richmond.gov.uk/libraries

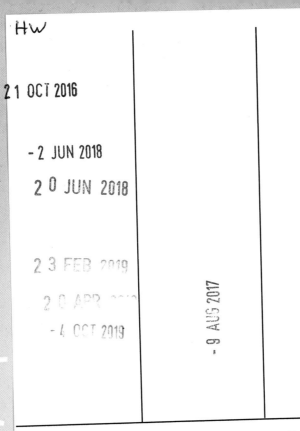

LONDON BOROUGH OF
RICHMOND UPON THAMES

First published 2016 by Walker Entertainment, an imprint of Walker Books Ltd
87 Vauxhall Walk, London SE11 5HJ

2 4 6 8 10 9 7 5 3 1

Text based on the script by Emma Hogan
Nelly & Nora is created by Gerard O'Rourke and developed by Emma Hogan
Illustrations from the TV animation produced by Geronimo Productions Ltd
Nelly & Nora original artwork and design by Emma Hogan
Licensed by Geronimo Productions Ltd © 2016

This book has been typeset in Baskerville.

Printed in China

British Library Cataloguing in Publication Data:
a catalogue record for this book is available from the British Library

ISBN 978-1-4063-5841-4

www.walker.co.uk

FSC
www.fsc.org

MIX
Paper from
responsible sources
FSC® C101537

Nelly & Nora

The Windy Way Home

WALKER
ENTERTAINMENT

Nelly and Nora are at the little beach
near the sand dunes.

They've spent the whole afternoon
building a cosy sand fort.

"Bunch up, Nelly!" says Nora, patting the sand beside her.

Nelly snuggles up to her sister and
together they lie back and look up at the sky.

Suddenly Nora gasps,
"Look, Nelly, look! The clouds are moving fast!"

"And look!
That bird is flying backwards!" says Nora.

"Oh!" says Nelly.
"It must be really windy up there!"

"Toooooo windy!" cries Nora.
"We should go home," says Nelly.

They run up the beach steps.

But at the top, the wind is very strong!

Nelly and Nora take   very   slow   steps,

but the wind pushes the girls back,
against the stone wall.

They try again.

"Oof!" Nora is blown onto the ground.

Then Nelly has an idea! She crouches down low.

"Let's crawl.
It's easier than walking in the wind!"

Nelly crawls faster than Nora ...

so Nora begins to roll along,
doing speedy somersaults.

Wheeeee!

It's lots of fun!

But soon the girls are dizzy and out of breath.
"I can't roll any more, Nelly!" pants Nora.
"Me neither," wheezes Nelly.

Nelly pulls a pack of carrot sticks from her pocket.
"Let's stop and feed the sheep!"

"Baaa," say the sheep loudly.
They like that plan!

The girls watch with surprise as the sheep
bunch up together and walk quickly towards them.

"Oh!" gasps Nelly.
"They bunched up to walk through the wind!"

They hear a loud "Chirp!" above.
The girls look up to see birds flying
together across the sky.

"They've bunched up too, Nelly!"
giggles Nora.
The girls look at each other.
"We should bunch up!"

Nelly and Nora snuggle up close
and begin to walk together.

But they're still   very   very   slow...

Suddenly they hear...

"Baaa!"

The sheep bunch up around Nelly and Nora,
helping them walk through the wind!

The girls giggle and laugh
as they move along with the sheep.

And together they make it all the way home!

"Good sheep!" says Nora, petting them.
"Thank you for helping us," says Nelly.

"Baaa," say the sheep.
Then, arm in arm, the girls go inside
and close the door on the very windy day.

Make four Nelly-and-Nora toy windmills!

Nelly and Nora had a very windy day.
Windmills can show how windy it is outside right now!
The faster the windmills spin, the stronger the wind.

Ask a grown-up to help!

YOU WILL NEED:
* a pair of scissors
* four pencils, all with erasers
* four drawing pins or pearl-headed pins

1. Remove the opposite page by tearing along the perforation. Carefully cut out the four squares along the dotted black lines.

2. Cut along the dotted white lines from the corners of each square. Don't cut all the way to the centres of the squares, though!

3. Pull the corners of each square over to the centre to form each windmill, like this:

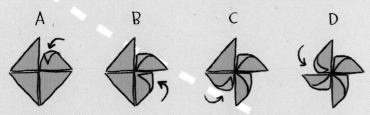

A   B   C   D

4. Line up the corners and stick a pin through them.

5. Now carefully stick the pin into the pencil eraser, like this:

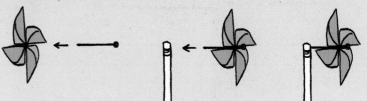

(Here's a tip: if you have a small bead, add it to the pin, between the windmill and the pencil eraser, for easier spinning.)

6. Ta-da! Blow on the windmills to test them out!

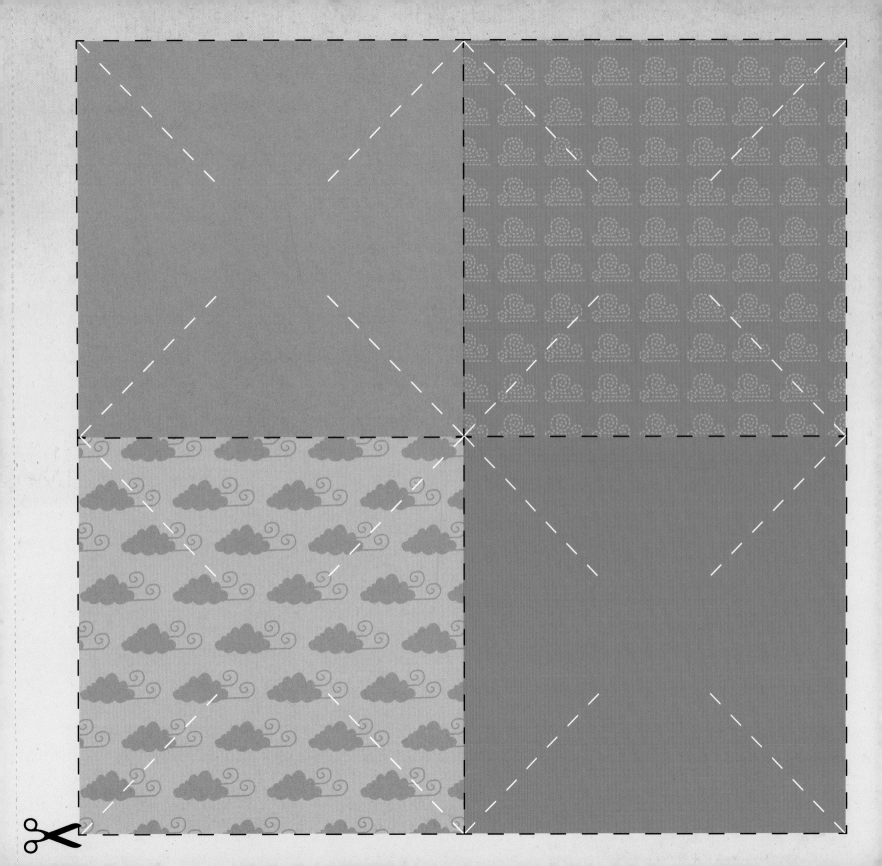

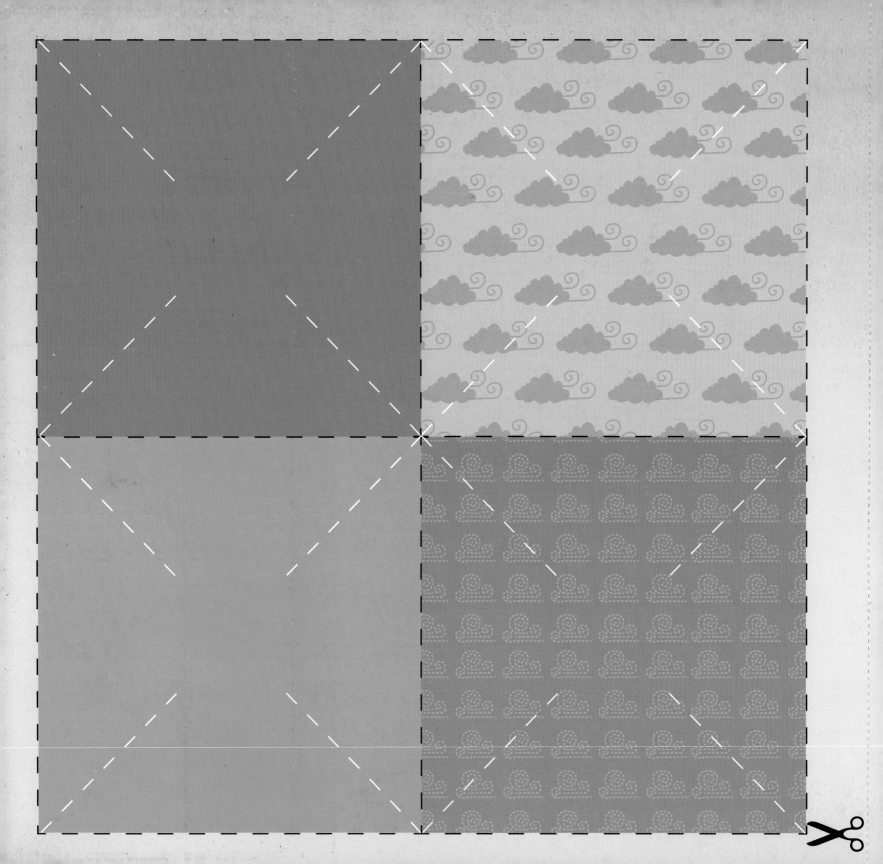